JACK JONES

THE LOST TEMPLE

ZANDER BINGHAM

GREEN RHINO
MEDIA

www.greenrhinomedia.com

First Printing: September 2018

Green Rhino Media LLC
228 Park Ave S
#15958
New York, NY 10003-1502
United States of America

www.jackjonesclub.com

ISBN 978-1-949247-02-2 *(Paperback - US)*

ISBN 978-1-949247-05-3 *(Paperback - UK/AU)*
ISBN 978-1-949247-08-4 *(eBook - US)*
ISBN 978-1-949247-11-4 *(eBook - UK/AU)*

Library of Congress Control Number: 2018954295

DEDICATION

This book is dedicated to my two
adventurous sons, Xavier and Greyson.
May your minds always be open.
Never stop learning and be forever curious.
Explore everywhere and
everything you can.

CONTENTS

DEDICATION.. iii

ACKNOWLEDGMENTS vi

CHAPTER ONE...1

CHAPTER TWO 13

CHAPTER THREE....................................... 26

CHAPTER FOUR 36

CHAPTER FIVE 46

CHAPTER SIX...57

CHAPTER SEVEN.. 68

CHAPTER EIGHT 82

TITLES IN THIS SERIES 97

ABOUT THE AUTHOR.............................. 98

ACKNOWLEDGMENTS

To my incredible wife, Diana, you are amazing. Thank-you for your help in bringing Jack Jones to life.

To my eldest son, Xavier, I could not have asked for a better audience to listen to the countless drafts of Jack's adventures. Your ideas, questions and input were invaluable.

To Kris, Allan, Felix and Gina, without your encouragement and support, this journey would simply not have been possible.

To Andrea, your illustrations brought us into Jack's world and enabled us to fully engage in the story and connect with the characters.

To Claire, your time and devotion, constructive feedback, attention to detail and real-world factoids helped maintain believability in an otherwise made-up story.

To friends and family members who have stuck by me in this new writing venture, please enjoy what your support has helped create.

CHAPTER ONE

"Just make sure you don't go trekking too far from the research site," instructed Mr. Jones, "the jungle around here is very dense and there are all sorts of dangers to look out for."

Jack, his sister, Emma, and best friend Albert all nodded as they packed the rest of their gear and prepared to head off on a hike.

"I know you three are very capable but please do be careful – and be sure to check-in with us if you have any trouble," added Mrs. Jones.

Theodore and Penelope Jones were professors of archaeology and history. They were leading a team of researchers excavating an ancient city that had just been discovered deep in the jungle.

Jack, Emma and Albert had joined them, and today they planned a hike through the area in search of adventure.

"Don't worry," Jack smiled back, "we'll look out for each other. That orienteering camp we went to last summer has prepared us for adventures exactly like this!"

"Plus, we've been hiking around this area all week with you and Dad, so we've got a handle on it," added Emma.

"Exactly!" agreed Jack, "I've got my tablet, so I can keep you updated as we go, *and* I brought my lucky jacket along, too!"

"Ah, what are all those dangers again?" asked Albert, a serious look on his face.

"Well, getting lost in the jungle is definitely a big concern, so keep your map and compass handy. Then there's the list of venomous snakes and spiders to watch out for. And don't be tempted to swim in any rivers, streams or lakes unless you're certain there are no piranhas..." Mr. Jones trailed off.

Jack patted Albert on the shoulder, "Thanks Dad, but Albert already knows all of this, he's just a little worried. I don't think hearing the list of all the things that could go wrong, *again*, will help him feel any better. And you know that I don't like snakes, so I'd rather not hear any more about those. I say we get going and make sure we keep our wits about us."

"Yes, Jack. I'm confident that you three have enough experience and sense to take a short trek like this safely. But I wouldn't be doing my job as your dad if I didn't point these things out," explained Mr. Jones with a warm smile.

Emma agreed, "Yeah, we'll stay together and make sure we take our time and be super careful."

"Alright, I suppose," groaned Albert.

"Come on, we've got all the gear we need – let's go exploring!" said Jack enthusiastically as he started off down one of the trails that led away from the excavation site.

"If you're not back by nightfall, we'll send out a search party!" Mrs. Jones called after them in a playful but serious voice.

"Remember to stick to the trails, and if you come across anything interesting, take photos and send them to Naomi for analysis," added Mr. Jones.

"Thanks Mom. Will do Dad!" said Jack, looking back and waving before disappearing into the thick jungle.

The sun was rising higher in the sky, though much of the light was blocked from reaching the jungle floor because of the dense green canopy overhead. The air was heavy, hot and humid as the three explorers walked further into the jungle.

Twigs crunched, branches snapped, and leaves shuffled beneath their feet as they went. An ever-present hum and buzz of insects and crawling creatures could be heard all around them.

"Wow, it sure is hot out here!" exclaimed Jack as they marched on through the jungle.

"No kidding... a swimming pool would be nice right about now," joked Albert as he wiped the sweat from his brow.

"Well, maybe we'll come across a lake or a river...?" Emma offered.

"Hmmm... what did your Dad say about piranhas in the lakes and rivers again?" asked Albert, his question dripping with sarcasm. "I've grown fond of my limbs just the way they are."

Jack laughed, "Well, I guess you can't have everything!"

Emma laughed, too, and eventually so did Albert.

The trio carried on trekking for quite some time and noticed the ground they'd been covering had been steadily inclining.

They stopped to snap pictures of colorful bugs and other interesting wildlife and plants.

Along the way, they came across a steep drop-off to their right with a valley and river below. They decided to follow along the edge of it, looking for a safe way to venture down to the valley floor.

"*Whew*, we've sure covered a lot of ground, and mostly uphill, too! How about we stop up there, at the base of that tree for a water break?" suggested Jack as he pointed to a large tree just ahead of them.

As they approached, they saw that the tree had a very wide trunk. On the ground, there were countless roots spanning out in all directions before disappearing down into the soil and over the side of the valley wall.

The tree was perched on the edge of the drop-off and if it weren't for all the heavy roots anchoring it in place, it looked as though it could tumble down the cliff at any moment.

Jack, Emma and Albert all found comfortable seats amongst the tree's roots and enjoyed some refreshing water in the shade.

A gentle breeze blew up from the valley below along with an interesting *whooshing* sound that caught everyone's attention.

Emma moved closer to the edge of the cliff. She stepped over the heavy tree roots and looked down.

"Wow, you both have to see this! There's a waterfall down here. It's coming out of the side of the cliff."

Jack and Albert made their way over to the ledge to check out Emma's discovery.

Albert's eyes lit up. "*Whoa!* It looks like there's a cave down there, too. And the waterfall is coming out the side of it...the water falls all the way down to the river."

Jack found a vantage spot, so he could see what Albert was talking about. It was spectacular.

Jack took some pictures with his tablet and admired the view.

"So cool! I've never seen anything quite like this. Hey, wouldn't it be awesome to see inside it?" Jack looked at Emma, then at Albert and grinned.

He surveyed the area around them, "Looks like it would be difficult to get down there though, we may have to come back with some climbing gear..." Jack's voice trailed off as he tried to think of a way to explore the cave below without needing to trek back to the camp.

"That would be awesome, JJ! Maybe we can find another way in, there could be another entrance further along the trail?" Emma was as keen as her brother.

Jack smiled and replied, "Great idea, Em! Come on, let's look around!"

CHAPTER TWO

Jack, Emma and Albert climbed back across
the large tree roots to explore more of the
area. As they made their way back to the path,
Albert tripped and stumbled over something
hidden on the jungle floor.

"Hey! Check this out!" exclaimed Albert as he
crouched down and began dusting leaves and
dirt out of the way to reveal the cause of his
stumble.

It was a circular rock that didn't look natural or like it ought to have been there. Jack and Emma crouched down and helped clear the stone's surface.

"There's some sort of symbol on it," Emma said, almost in a whisper.

"You're right, this does look interesting, and definitely man-made. I'll take a photo and send it to Naomi, perhaps she can tell us what it means."

Jack retrieved his tablet from his backpack, snapped a photo and sent it to Naomi with a quick message:

Hey Naomi, stumbled across this in the jungle, wondering if you can tell us more about it? Thanks, Jack.

Naomi was Mr. and Mrs. Jones' research assistant, and good friend, who was always happy to help Jack, Emma and Albert solve a mystery. Her interest in all things historical meant that she was a terrific resource. She was always able to find the information they needed and answer the questions they had.

The symbol looked like it came from a time long ago. It was round with smaller symbols etched around a central figure that looked like a face. There were two swirl cut-outs for eyes.

The nose appeared to be a set of stairs that led up to the entrance of some sort of temple, and there was a mouth that had boulders for teeth.

A waterfall pouring from the mouth symbolized a tongue.

"How neat! I wonder if there are any more like it around?" said Albert.

"Yeah, I wonder. Why don't we hunt around and see what else we can find?" replied Jack.

"Let's keep following along the edge of the cliff until we're right over where the waterfall is coming out. Come on!"

Jack stood, and together they kept walking along the trail which was still heading uphill.

They trekked toward where they had seen the waterfall, though at a slower pace so they could examine the ground for more hidden relics.

The group walked and searched a little longer before they all stopped.

Suddenly, they looked at one another curiously, and it was obvious they were all feeling the same strange thing.

"Do you feel that?" asked Jack.

"And *hear* that?" added Emma.

The ground beneath them rumbled ever so slightly and there was another faint whooshing sound.

As they searched for the source, the sound and rumbling stopped. Jack's tablet pinged drawing their attention to it.

"That's probably Naomi, wow, she's fast!" said Jack as he pulled his tablet out of his backpack, opening the message and reading it aloud to the others.

Hello Jack,

This is a very interesting find indeed!

That symbol you have discovered is very rare and only referenced in a few of the records discovered from that era.

It is believed to be the symbol used for a very special place known as the Temple of the Underworld.

It was one of the most sacred temples of its time. Referred to in some records as 'the hidden temple', it is believed to have been constructed in secret and only the high priests and priestesses knew of its location.

Archaeologists have searched for the temple on several expeditions over the years but have never found any trace of it.

Some believe that it is only a legend.

Others though, believe it is where the most important high priests and priestesses were entombed.

The temple is also said to house a very important, (and so far, never located) artifact known as the Book of the Gods.

As far as I could determine, that stone symbol you found is the only physical evidence of the temple ever actually discovered.

I'm going to forward a picture of it to your parents as well. It may be a marker or some sort of ancient sign post.

I would suggest investigating further, and please let me know if you find anything – I'm very curious about this one, and I think the team working with your parents will be, too!

"You mean there could be a lost temple somewhere around here?" Emma blurted, barely able to contain her excitement.

"It sure sounds like it! I wonder what's in this *Book of the Gods*?" Albert pondered.

Jack was about to reply when they all heard the thunderous crack of heavy stone breaking beneath them.

A huge slab of rock angled downward, creating a long ramp into a deep cavern below.

Before they had a chance to react, the ground fell out from under their feet, and Jack, Emma and Albert began to fall.

They slid down along the ramp, the slippery mud and leaves making it impossible to stop themselves until they reached the bottom. They came to a halt in a mucky pile of rocks, leaves and mud.

Feeling a little dazed and disoriented the three hikers stood up, dusted themselves off and checked for any injuries.

Then they heard it, another deafening crack echoed around the cavern.

"Run!" yelled Jack as he huddled Emma and Albert away from the noise and took shelter behind a large boulder sitting on the ground.

The large stone slab, which had been leaning as a ramp to the surface, fell with an almighty crash to the ground below, breaking into smaller boulders and rocks as it filled the air with dust and debris.

Jack, Emma and Albert cautiously peeked over the boulder they'd sheltered behind. Seeing that the debris was starting to settle, they all stood-up and walked back out toward the open area of the cave.

"Is everyone alright?" Jack asked.

"I'm fine... just a bit muddy," replied Emma.

"I think I'm alright. I'm muddy too, but everything's still attached," joked Albert, "but *now* where are we?"

CHAPTER THREE

The cave was enormous. Lots of rocks and boulders were scattered around from where the roof had collapsed, leaving a large opening in the ceiling.

A river flowed through the middle of the cave then out through an opening in the side.

Dust surrounded the three friends in a thick cloud, still heavy in the air from the collapse, making it dark and difficult to see.

Following the light, Jack, Emma and Albert walked over to the side opening and looked out from the cliff face.

"Well, JJ, you were saying you wanted to find where this waterfall was coming from," said Emma, grinning excitedly, "I think this is it!"

"That's true. I guess we've answered that question *and* figured out another way in!" laughed Jack.

"The trouble now is, how do we find a way *out*?" added Albert.

"Good point Albert, it's a long way up to the opening we fell through. We can take a closer look once the dust settles back there, but from what I could see the walls didn't really look too climbable. And we didn't bring any gear for that."

"Yeah, we sure weren't expecting to need any climbing equipment today," said Albert.

He pointed to the corner closest to them, "Are those stairs?"

"Hmmm, that's interesting. It looks like there used to be a staircase here that went up the cliffside to the top of the valley…"

Jack observed that there were only a few steps still left sticking out of the cliff, the rest had fallen away. "It sure is a long way down from up there."

"I guess we can't get back up that way, then. It also means that we're not the first or only people to have been here! Building stairs on the side of a cliff into a cave isn't something you do for no reason," said Albert, contemplating their accidental discovery.

"You're right! Maybe there's more to this cave than we realize. And don't worry about getting out of here, we can just call my parents on my tablet and they will come with more gear and help us climb out... I was holding it when we fell in here and must have dropped it on the way down," Jack's voice trailed off.

The boys began looking around for the tablet when Emma announced, "Jack! Albert! you've got to see this!"

They turned around to see what Emma was talking about. The sight before them was incredible.

Most of the dust had settled now. The air had cleared, and light poured in from the opening overhead and through the side.

Now they were able take in the vast size of the cave, and even more remarkable was what appeared to be a large stone temple on an island in the center of the cave. It stretched back as far as they could see into the darkness.

There were statues and intricate carvings all around the cave walls and even more on the temple itself.

Some areas had been damaged by the roof caving in, but much of the cave, and the impressive structures within it, still looked to be intact.

The cave seemed very old, and there were even large tree roots coming into the cave ceiling from above, searching for water.

They had attached themselves to the rocky walls as they snaked their way downward.

Emma pointed to the top of the temple, "Look! That's the same symbol Albert found by the big tree! Do you think this is the temple Naomi told us about... the *Temple of the Underworld*?"

"That makes sense, for sure," nodded Jack, "it kind of feels like we *are* under the world down here! The symbols match. Plus, being hidden in this cave would explain why it hasn't ever been found before."

"Remember those broken stairs we found near the waterfall when we first fell into the cave?" asked Albert, "They must have led up to the stone symbol I tripped over earlier. Maybe it was like a marker, so the priests could find it?"

"Right!" Jack agreed, "So... how about we see if we can find the *Book of the Gods* while we're here?"

Emma clapped her hands together eagerly, "JJ, that's a great idea!"

"I'm in, too," grinned Albert, "but first let's tell your parents where we are and what we think we've found... so we don't end up lost down here for hundreds of years like this temple!"

"Good thinking," replied Jack as he walked back into the cave, searching for his tablet. "It must be around somewhere."

After a short search and shifting rocks aside, Jack found it.

"Hmmm, this isn't so good... it's been completely smashed by the rocks. The screen is broken, and it won't turn on!" Jack frowned as he pushed the power button a few more times, hoping it might start up again. It didn't.

"Well," said Albert as he surveyed the area, "the stairs are missing, and I agree that there doesn't really seem to be a way to climb back *up* and out of here, hmmm..."

"I guess we'll just need to find another way, then," replied Emma, matter-of-factly.

Albert watched as the water flowed quickly past them on its way toward the waterfall, "You know, this water must be coming in here from *somewhere*. What if we follow it upstream and see if there's a way out?"

Jack nodded and gave Albert a pat on the shoulder, "Good idea! Perhaps we won't be stuck down here forever after all!"

"But I think we should see what's at the top of the temple first," said Emma, "We might just find the *Book of the Gods*. Wouldn't that be cool?"

Jack looked up toward the temple, "Since we're here already, I agree, let's get to the top and see what we find. From there we can figure out what to do next. Come on, follow me!"

The route to the base of the temple was strewn with boulders, rocks and dust that crunched beneath their feet as the trio began making their way further into the cave.

CHAPTER FOUR

The river flowed into the cavern from behind the temple. It then separated into two streams that ran around either side of the temple before joining again in front and continuing to eventually become the waterfall that flowed out of the cave.

"*Cool!* The way this river flows all around the temple kind of makes it an island in the middle," said Jack.

"Yeah, like a moat around a castle. Only there's no drawbridge," added Emma.

"I'd say they built it that way on purpose," said Albert, "Look over here, where the streams meet in front of the temple. There are stepping stones to get across to the island, or to cross over to the other side of the cavern."

Glancing into the river, Jack eyed the large, smooth, circular stones warily, "I wonder how long it's been since someone has used any of these?"

"I'd say...a *really* long time," answered Albert, "See over there? A few of them have already sunk below the surface or toppled over."

The water churned and bubbled between the stones as Jack cautiously placed one foot onto the nearest stone and applied some pressure to it.

"Don't fall in – remember there could be piranhas in this river, Jack!" Emma called out to her brother.

Just then, the stone beneath Jack's foot began to sink. Jack quickly shifted his weight back to the other foot and regained his balance. The stone continued to sink below the surface of the fast-moving water.

"These sinking stones aren't the answer," joked Jack, "I think we'll need to find another way across."

The river was too wide to jump over, and they couldn't walk through without soaking themselves and their gear, or risk being swept away and over the waterfall. And they certainly didn't want to be attacked by any piranhas that could be lurking in the dark water!

"We could try a few of the other stones, let's see if any of those are in better condition," suggested Albert.

The three explorers tried the stepping stones reachable from the riverbank, but they all sank quickly when stood on. They were not stable enough to provide a safe path across to the island.

"Hmmm... what else is around here that we can use, anyone bring a pogo stick?" giggled Jack.

Emma chuckled at the thought of the three children bouncing across the river on pogo sticks.

"Let's split up and look around this cave. There must be a way to cross the river and get over to the temple," said Albert.

The trio went in different directions to see what they could find. They began in the front area of the cave, because it was much darker toward the back, where the light from the ceiling collapse and side-wall openings couldn't reach.

"I haven't found anything over here. Any luck Albert?" Jack called out.

"Nothing here either, that is unless we have enough time to build a new bridge out of all these rocks!" Albert called back.

Jack laughed, "Hopefully we can find a faster way than that! How about you, Em?"

"I think I have an idea!" Emma said as she studied the tree roots growing down into the cave.

"Look, these tree roots go all the way up to the top of the cave. If we could pull them away from the wall then we could use them to swing over the river," said Emma.

She climbed up onto a large boulder, reached up and started to pull at one of the roots attached to the wall.

"That's a great idea!" Jack replied, and he climbed up to help.

It was well attached, but once Albert joined in, they made good progress. Soon they had a strong and stable tree root dangling onto the floor, perfectly positioned to swing across the river where they could access the temple.

Not wanting it to get snagged on something, Jack used a jungle knife from his backpack to cut the root, so it no longer dragged on the ground.

He pulled downward a few times to make sure it was secure.

"This doesn't feel like it's going anywhere, and it holds me without any problems," Jack said backing up and preparing for a running jump.

"I'll go first to make sure it's safe," volunteered Jack.

He clutched the root and started running toward the river. Just as Jack neared the river's edge, he lifted his feet from the ground and raised his legs as he swung effortlessly through the air, over the river and landed with a *thud* on the other side.

"*Woo!* That was cool! Now it's your turn, Em!" said Jack as he swung the tree root back across the river.

Emma grabbed hold of the swinging vine and began to run toward the river's edge. *"Weeee!"* she shouted as she swung easily across before passing it back to Albert.

"Ready or not, here I come!" Albert yelled as he ran, clearing the river and landing on the other side with his friends.

He then rolled a large rock over the top of the root to hold it in place on the temple side of the river.

They weren't sure what awaited them, but if they had to return the same way, they'd be able to swing back across.

"Awesome, you two!" Jack said as he high-fived Emma and Albert, "Now, let's explore this temple."

CHAPTER FIVE

Jack, Emma and Albert gazed up at the temple before them in wonder. Now that they were closer, the full size and grandeur was even more spectacular than before.

There had been more damage to it than they realized. Many stones had fallen out of the structure, making access to the interior more difficult.

"How do you suppose they managed to build something like this down here, inside a cave?" Emma asked, still bewildered.

Albert nodded his head and replied, "It really is amazing that something like this exists, it must have taken a *lot* of people a *very* long time to build it."

Albert thought back to Mrs. Ark's history class, where they learned about ancient civilizations and some of the incredible structures they were able to build before machines were invented.

Jack started walking slowly around the area, looking for a way inside. "Getting in may be a challenge. It looks like most of the entrance has fallen in. Come on, let's take a closer look."

Jack began walking up the stairs toward the entrance, dodging the larger pieces of fallen rocks that lay around.

When he reached the top of the stairs he found that most of the front entrance had completely collapsed and there didn't appear to be a way in.

"I don't know that we'll be able to get through this way," said Jack as he looked around.

"I think you're right, Jack," agreed Albert, "these rocks are too big to move. And it looks like when the roof collapsed, some of the falling rocks completely sealed this entrance. Maybe it's a sign from the *'Underworld Gods'* that we shouldn't go in?"

"Or maybe only those who try hard enough will be able to find a way," said Emma as she began climbing up the rocks to look for a way inside.

"Be careful up there!" Jack warned as she scampered up the debris and out of sight.

A few moments later Emma reappeared but with a disappointed look on her face, "I couldn't find any way through, just rocks, rocks and more rocks up here."

"Alright, let's start checking the sides of the temple, perhaps we'll have more luck there," said Jack.

As Emma began to climb down, some of the rocks shifted beneath her feet causing her to slide down amongst an avalanche of falling rubble and stones.

"Ahhh!" she cried as she tumbled back down to the ground.

"Em, are you alright?" asked Jack as he and Albert rushed over.

Emma was sitting on the ground surrounded by rocks and dust, "I think so..." she replied, looking at her arms and legs and wiggling her fingers.

"I think you were lucky," said Jack grimly as he looked her over for any sign of injury.

"Yeah, I know! I guess my gymnastics lessons are no match for ancient temple ruins. I've got a few scratches and scrapes, and there'll probably be some bruises show up soon, but I'm fine," assured Emma.

Jack reached out his hand and helped pull his sister to her feet again. "Are you still up to finding a way into the temple?"

Emma smiled, "Sure I am! I'm no quitter, and I'm not going to let you guys have all the fun!"

"We need to be very careful. If one of us gets badly hurt it will be even more difficult to get out of here," said Albert.

"You're right. This place is old, and these stones are heavy! I wouldn't want any of us to end up squashed under one of them!"

"It gets darker down the sides of the temple, as we get further away from the openings in the cave, let's get our flashlights out," Albert suggested.

The trio grabbed flashlights from their backpacks and started moving slowly along the left side of the temple, heading further into the cave.

The air felt cooler and was a welcome change from the heat of the jungle.

Albert shone his flashlight along the side wall of the temple. "Looks like there are some narrow rectangular openings along the sides, like windows, but not wide enough for us to get through."

"Nice spotting! Maybe there are some bigger ones or even a broken one that's wider," replied Jack.

They continued trekking further toward the back of the cave.

The river babbled and gurgled to their left, the temple towered above them on their right.

As they reached the back corner of the temple, Albert, who had been studying the walls with his flashlight called out to the others, "Over here, this might be something!"

"What is it, Albert?" asked Emma.

Albert walked closer to the wall shining his flashlight on a large gap. "It looks like some of the wall has broken away here, perhaps we can climb in through that hole."

Jack joined Emma and Albert, and all three shone their flashlights through the hole and found that they could see all the way inside. From where they were, though, it wasn't possible to know just *what* type of room it was.

"Great find, Albert!" said Jack, "Let's check it out!"

Jack began climbing over the pile of rocks that had broken out of the wall and very carefully crawled through the opening.

He brushed a lot of thick cobwebs out of the way and stood up again once he was inside. He looked around the dark space.

"What do you see, Jack?" Emma called out impatiently.

"Is it safe?" asked Albert.

Jack didn't reply right away, Emma and Albert looked at each other nervously.

"Jack! Are you alright?"

Jack called back, his voice echoing off the walls from inside the temple, "Ah, yeah... it's safe, just prepare yourselves though, I think I found the bone room!"

"Wait a minute, did he say *'throne room'*?" asked Albert, turning toward Emma.

Emma, looking equally confused, just shrugged.

CHAPTER SIX

Emma climbed through the opening in the wall first, followed by Albert. As she looked around the room with her flashlight, she let out a squeal, causing Albert to bump his head as he clambered through the opening.

"*Ouch!* What is it, Em?" Albert asked as he entered the room, rubbing his head where he'd bumped it.

"Are you alright?" Jack asked.

"Yes, I'm fine, but what is Emma squealing at?"

"Take a look for yourself."

Jack shone his flashlight toward the far wall and then swept it back and forth from one end of the long room to the other.

"Oh...*whoa!* You said *bone* room, not *throne* room!" Albert gasped as he took in the sight.

"And it's like this all the way around the room," added Jack, "I guess we're lucky we didn't crawl into one of *them!*"

The room they had entered was long and rectangular. Shelves had been built all along the stone walls, three rows high.

Skeletons lay on the shelves, separated by rectangular stones placed between the feet of one and the skull of the next. There were at least fifty skeletons, each decorated with elaborate jewels. The gold and precious gems glistened colorfully as the flashlights scanned over them.

"Looks as though Naomi was right. This must be where they entombed the dead priests and priestesses," said Albert, taking in their marvelous discovery.

"I've never seen anything like this before!" said Emma, admiring the craftsmanship of the stonework, and the beauty of the jewels.

"It's awesome, right? I think we should explore the rest of the temple and see what else there is! If we found this, maybe we can find the *Book of the Gods*, too?" said Jack excitedly and he began heading toward the far end of the room.

"Alright! Let's try to be quick though. I don't think I want to spend the night in here," cautioned Albert, eyeing the bony company around them.

"*Eww*, I agree!" giggled Emma.

Jack led the way through a passage at the far end of the crypt. It opened into a large square room with a high stone ceiling and a large firepit in the middle.

Ahead of them, they saw the inside of the collapsed entrance, and there were passageways leading to additional areas on both the left and right sides of the room.

"Let's check this room out first, then we can investigate the others," said Jack, shining his flashlight around.

"There's some logs by this firepit over here, maybe we can get the fire started?" suggested Albert. He picked up a few logs from the pile and grabbed some kindling that lay next to the fire pit.

"Good thinking, Albert!" replied Jack.

Albert took a flint from his backpack and lit the kindling. Small flames began to crackle and soon, the large logs began to burn, dramatically filling the temple with light and heat.

"Look at all the carvings!" exclaimed Emma as the orange light from the fire flickered across the walls.

"It's magical." She paused for a moment to imagine the temple at the height of its glory, "What do you suppose all of these symbols and carvings mean?"

"Great question, Em! We'll need to get Mom and Dad down here with their team to look at it and decipher it all. It really does seem like this was a very important place, ... if only I had my tablet, I could take pictures to show them."

"They are definitely going to be very excited to see this!" added Albert.

"Let's take a look in these other rooms. How about we start with the one on the right?" said Jack, heading toward the passageway.

"Sounds good to me," Albert replied, as he and Emma followed closely behind Jack.

The trio explored the next area. There was a firepit in the middle of the room but no wood, so they stuck to their flashlights instead. This new room was smaller than the main chamber, with more elaborate carvings and paintings on its walls. On the rear wall was what appeared to be a map of the area. The three walked over to study it more closely.

"I think this is where we are, here. And this looks like the waterfall coming out of the cave we fell into... and there's the temple," said Emma, pointing to a section near the center of the map.

"That makes sense," replied Jack, "and this city over here is a similar shape to the ruins of the dig site Mom and Dad are working on."

"Oh, yeah!" agreed Albert. "It looks like there were a few different structures built around this area. I wonder what all these lines are that go between them? They look like roads."

"Hmmm" said Jack, "They do *look* like roads, but we didn't see any when we were exploring in the jungle. Maybe they're overgrown now?"

"Yeah, that's possible, all these ruins *are* very old. Three roadways all heading in different directions and with symbols on top of them, too. Look at this one! I've seen this before at the dig site... very interesting... all three roads appear to begin behind the temple we're in," observed Albert.

"Maybe there is a way out from there?" Emma suggested.

"There could be! I think we should check out the room on the other side of the main chamber first, then we'll go and look."

"Good idea. Let's go!" said Albert and they all left the map room, excited to explore the other side of the temple.

CHAPTER SEVEN

Jack, Emma and Albert ran back to the main chamber of the temple and across to the other passageway, excited to see what they might find.

Jack's foot snagged something as they entered, tripping him up a little as the object flung across the stone floor.

"What was that, Jack?" asked Emma.

"Not sure…" Jack shone his flashlight toward the floor. "Careful, there are broken pieces of stone scattered all over here."

All three explored the area with their flashlights. The room was the same size as the map room. There was a firepit in the middle, as well as the remains of a collapsed stone staircase.

Its crumbled steps were scattered around the floor in the back of the room.

Jack shone his flashlight up toward the ceiling along the back wall and saw an open space in the roof. "It looks like this is how we get to the level above us! Or at least how they did before the stairs collapsed. If the book is still here, I reckon that's where we'll find it!"

"I think we should definitely take a look... but getting up there without the stairs presents a challenge," said Albert.

Jack nodded, "We'll work out a way. We've solved bigger problems than this. Come on, let's look around and see what we can use to get up there."

With their flashlights, they searched for a way to reach the upper level.

It was quite high and there wasn't anything around to stand on.

"I've got an idea!" said Jack thoughtfully. He placed his backpack down on the floor and retrieved a small coil of rope from it.

"What are you going to do?" asked Emma.

Jack pointed his flashlight upward, where the stairs had originally joined the upper and lower levels. He showed Emma and Albert a piece of stone that jutted out from the edge.

"We don't have all of our climbing gear, but I do have some rope. I'm going to hook it over that piece of stone up there and then use it to climb up the wall. Can you both shine your flashlights up there while I toss the rope up?"

"Why, sure we can, Sheriff!" said Albert in his best cowboy voice. He and Emma giggled as they shone their flashlights up toward the stone.

Jack prepared his rope and threw it up and over the beam. He managed to hook the beam on his first go! He then secured it and held on tight as he used the rope to support himself as he walked up the wall.

"Yee-haw! Maybe I could be a cowboy!" joked Jack.

"Nice work, Jack!" said Emma, "We'll follow you up."

When Jack reached the top, he carefully pulled himself up and onto the second level before turning around and calling down, "I've made it. Come on up!"

Emma was next to climb up the wall. Once she was at the top, Jack reached out to help pull her up onto the platform.

It was Albert's turn. When he was about halfway up, the block of stone that held the rope began to shift.

"Yikes! Be careful, Albert!" yelled Jack, as he grabbed hold of the rope, in case the stone wobbled out of place.

"Sh-should I go back down?" stuttered Albert.

"I've got you," Jack said through clenched teeth. He clutched the rope, supporting his friend, "keep coming, you'll make it!"

After a few tense moments, and some minor rope burn on Jack's hands, they helped pull Albert up onto the platform. *Phew!* The trio high-fived one another, relieved to have made it up safely.

The upper level of the temple was built out of stone like the rest of the structure, only instead of narrow windows, there were wide square columns separated by gaps, which let in more light from the cave openings.

The cave itself was already starting to get dark as the sun sank in the afternoon sky, so the area was poorly lit. Jack, Emma and Albert shone their flashlights around the space to get a better sense of what was there. They found fire pits in each corner of the rectangular room and a stone altar in the middle.

Jack shone his light onto the surface of the altar and began walking toward it. "Do you think this could be what we've been searching for?" he said, glancing across the altar at Emma and Albert.

Suddenly, Jack froze as an unwelcome sound could be heard behind him.

"Sssssssss"

Emma and Albert backed away, acting quickly to help Jack.

"Please don't tell me there's a s-s-snake…"

"It's ok, Jack," Albert assured his friend.

He quickly recalled a lesson from zoology camp – snakes were attracted to heat! Albert sprang into action. "Emma, use my flint and the kindling to light the fire in that pit there with the logs in it. We can use the flames to attract the snake's attention and spook it away."

"Don't move until we say, Jack!" said Albert, firmly but calmly.

"*O-K,*" moaned Jack, "but please hurry!" Jack was a born adventurer, but there was just one thing he couldn't handle – snakes!

Thanks to the very dry wood, and Albert's flint, the fire grew quickly. Then, Emma and Albert carefully picked up a flaming log each and began waving them at the snake.

There were beams running across the top of the ceiling, and the snake, not seeming to like the fire logs being waved at it, quickly recoiled itself around the beam before slithering away and out of sight.

"*Phew!* Thanks so much. You both did an awesome job solving that slithery problem!" sighed Jack, relieved the snake was gone.

Emma and Albert felt rather heroic and the three of them chuckled, glad that the situation was under control.

"It was tough to tell for sure, but I reckon that was a python – it was *huge!*" said Albert, expanding his arms fully to indicate the size of the slithering reptile.

"I think I've heard enough, let's keep a better look out from now on, OK?" replied Jack.

The trio gathered around the altar and peered at the large, very old book that sat in the middle. It was made from thin tree bark and felt almost velvety to the touch.

"We should be very careful not to damage anything. This has been undisturbed here for a very long time," cautioned Albert as they looked over the cover, observing the characters and colors that were still remarkably vivid.

"You're right," agreed Jack.

He ran his hand softly over the cover and gently began to peel it open. It felt very fragile.

"Maybe we should take this with us rather than risk damaging it here."

"I think that's a good plan!" replied Emma.

"Can you believe we've found an historical artifact that proper archaeologists have been searching *years* to find?"

"I know! So neat," replied Albert, "Hey, while we're here, I think it might be cool to sketch a map of this temple, so we can note all the rooms we found and show it to your parents and the excavation team."

"Brilliant idea, Albert!" Emma and Jack both agreed.

They worked to carefully store the book safely in Jack's backpack, while Albert grabbed a notepad and pencil and began to draw a map of the temple and all the areas they'd been exploring.

Just as they had latched up Jack's backpack, and Albert had wrapped up his map sketching, a very loud cracking sound echoed around the chamber and they felt the ground beneath them shake.

Then, with a mighty *crash*, another large section of rock fell from above.

"Oh, not again," groaned Albert.

"Quick! Get under here!" yelled Jack as he ushered Emma and Albert to safety beneath the stone altar.

CHAPTER EIGHT

The clattering, crashing and crumbling sounds lasted for what felt like an eternity. The echo inside the cave was deafening and the three adventurers could feel their hearts racing, concerned that the roof may fall in on them.

Finally, quiet returned and the only sounds that could be heard were their rapid breathing and the flow of the river babbling by outside the temple.

"Are you both alright?" asked Jack, catching his breath and sounding relieved.

"*Whew!* That was intense," replied Emma, gripping her chest, "but yeah, I'm alright."

"Intense? I'll say! I'm fine, Jack, but I definitely think we should find a way out of here before anything else falls down!" added Albert.

Jack and Emma both nodded in agreement. The three climbed out from under the altar. As they stood, they began looking around to assess where the rocks had fallen from and if there was any new damage. Jack and Emma looked out the windows.

The air was still cloudy with dust which made it difficult to see far beyond the temple.

But now there was a much larger opening in the roof of the cave than before.

Albert went to look at the area they had climbed up from, "I don't think we're going to be able to go back the way we came. It looks as though some of the cave roof landed on the room we came up through and now it's crushed."

"I have an idea," said Jack as he headed over to the side of the room closest to the recent collapse.

"I think our best chance is to climb out of here between these pillars. We can then make our way over the roof that hasn't been damaged and then climb down the rubble pile, using it like a ramp."

Albert and Emma were following along the proposed route as Jack explained his plan.

"I get your idea," said Emma, "but we'll need to make sure we don't go causing any avalanches. The last rock pile I went climbing on wasn't very safe."

"Alright! I'll go first," said Jack. "It might be safer to wait until I get all the way down, then follow me one at a time – *slowly*!" advised Jack as he began to climb out through the pillars.

Jack made his way onto the roof and then stepped carefully along the narrow ledge leading to the recently collapsed area of the temple.

The most dangerous part of his descent was climbing down the unstable rocks and rubble to the ground. He paid attention to where he stepped and took his time.

After only a couple of minor slips and a few issues with some rolling rocks, he was down.

Emma went next, followed by Albert. Both took their time and met Jack safely on the ground.

By this stage the dust had settled, and the larger opening in the cave roof as well as the damage to the temple was easier to see.

Most of the temple was still intact, however the three of them agreed that if more large pieces of the cave roof were to come down, it would cause significant destruction.

"Hmmmm, this latest rock fall hasn't made it any easier for us to get out! We're still going to need to find another way," said Jack.

"I've been thinking about that!" replied Albert thoughtfully, "Do you remember those lines we saw on the map? We thought they were roads but wondered why we didn't see any sign of them as we were trekking in the jungle."

"Yes, I remember..." said Jack, "so if they aren't roads, what do you think they could be?"

"What if they were *tunnels*?" replied Albert, grinning excitedly.

"Tunnels? That would be great! There were lines on that map leading to the ruins Mom and Dad are working on. What if we could follow a tunnel right to them?" exclaimed Emma.

"That's right!" replied Albert with a smile, "I think we should go to the back of the cave, where the river flows in, and see what we can find there."

"Alright, let's go!"

Jack led Emma and Albert back to the tree root they had used earlier, taking turns to swing back across the river.

From there they made their way quickly to the very back of the cave and began to look around. They found a stone path that followed along the side of the river and led to an opening in the back wall of the cave.

"It looks like the temple builders intended for people to come through here. Kind of like a trail. You might just be on to something Albert!" said Jack as he surveyed the path.

"Look up there, it's another waterfall!" Emma called to the boys. "It's spectacular!"

There was a round opening extending up to the surface where water gushed down, splashing into a small pool. The *whooshing* of water echoed off the walls loudly.

"Oh, so this is where the water comes into the cave and forms the underground river that surrounds the temple!" observed Albert. "

Jack studied the area briefly. "It would be difficult to climb up here, especially with all that water flowing down. Let's keep going."

The three explorers ventured further into the cave, their flashlights illuminating the way as they walked. Eventually they came to an alcove with three passageways, all leading in different directions.

There was a symbol above each one. Thinking back to the map inside the temple Jack said, "I'm pretty sure the right tunnel was the one that led to Mom and Dad's site."

"I agree," said Albert, "plus the symbol above matches the one they keep finding on the buildings at the dig your parents are working on!"

"Perfect! Right it is! The map we found on the wall in the temple should help them to find the other sites that must be around here somewhere, too," said Emma happily.

Even she was glad they were on their way back to the safety of the camp.

The tunnel was in remarkably good condition, with intricate carvings and ancient artwork painted along the way. The time passed quickly as the trio trekked through the tunnel. They talked excitedly about their discovery and enjoyed playing echo games, yelling out into the vast darkness of the tunnel.

Suddenly they heard scraping sounds, like heavy stones grinding across each other.

"Oh, please not another collapse!" shrieked Albert.

Then, a ray of light pierced the darkness of the tunnel in front of them and Jack, Emma and Albert heard voices.

"Hello? Is anyone down there?" came the sound of a familiar voice from further down the tunnel.

"Dad, is that you?" Jack called back.

"Yes, Jack! What are you doing down here?"

"It's a long story, but we think you're going to like it!" replied Jack, excitedly.

And with that, Jack, Emma and Albert ran to the tunnel opening where a very happy Mr. and Mrs. Jones greeted them.

"We heard noises coming from down here and shifted some old stones out of the way to see what was going on. That's when we discovered this tunnel entrance," explained Mrs. Jones.

"Oh, it's so wonderful to see you all!" she said as she cuddled Emma and ruffled the boys' hair.

Over a campfire dinner that evening, Jack strummed his guitar in tune with the vibrant sounds of the surrounding jungle.

Later, as they toasted marshmallows, Jack, Emma and Albert told the story of how they fell into the *Temple of the Underworld*, found the *Book of the Gods* and escaped through an ancient tunnel.

Mr. and Mrs. Jones and all the archaeologists working on the site could barely believe what they heard. They were completely amazed that the three explorers had returned with such an important, historical artifact.

They discussed who best to entrust with the *Book of the Gods* and it was agreed that such a sought-after relic belonged in a museum.

Everyone was very excited to explore the newly discovered temple and had already begun planning. The expedition to the underground site would be led by Jack, Emma and Albert.

"You are all intrepid adventurers indeed! Not too many have ventured to the *underworld* and returned to tell the tale!" joked Mr. Jones.

Everyone laughed.

THE END

TITLES IN THIS SERIES

COMING SOON

The Desert Quest   The Mysterious Light

Castle on the Cliff   The Ghost Ship

www.jackjonesclub.com

ABOUT THE AUTHOR

Zander Bingham was born and raised on a boat. It was captured by pirates when he was just 12-years-old. He, along with his family and crew, swam to a nearby island where Zander spent his days imagining swashbuckling adventures on the high seas.

Well, not exactly.

But Zander did love boating adventures as a kid. And he always dreamed of exploring deserted islands and being a real-life castaway. He grew up cruising around Australia, the USA and The Bahamas. He eventually captained his very own sail boat, living aboard and exploring the Adriatic Sea with his wife and two young sons.

His thirst for exploration, his witty sense of humor, and his new-found passion for writing stories to read to his boys at bedtime, led to the creation of Jack Jones; the confident, brave and curious boy adventurer who is always searching for his next escapade.

CPSIA information can be obtained
at www.ICGtesting.com
Printed in the USA
LVHW011255160820
663166LV00002B/3